The Three Little Pigs

Modern Curriculum Press
BEGINNING TO READ Series

Margaret Hillert

The Three Little Pigs

illustrated by Irma Wilde

MODERN CURRICULUM PRESS
Cleveland • Toronto

ISBN 0-8136-5535-8 (paperback)
ISBN 0-8136-5035-6 (hardbound)

1 2 3 4 5 6 7 8 9 10 91 92

Here is a pig.

Here is a pig.

And here is a pig.

One, two, three.

Three little pigs.

Three funny little pigs.

See my house.

It is a little house.

It is yellow.

Little pig, little pig.

I want to come in.

You can not.

You can not.

You can not come in.

I can puff the house down.

Puff, puff, puff.

Here is my house.

It is a funny little house.

Little pig, little pig.

I want to come in.

You can not.

You can not.

You can not come in.

See me puff, puff, puff.

I can puff the house down.

Look here, look here.

My house is a big one.

It is red.

Little pig, little pig.

I want to come in.

Go away.

Go away.

You can not come in.

See me puff.

I can puff.

I can puff the house down.

See here, see here.

My house is not down.

I can go up, up, up.

I can go in.

Oh my, oh my.

It is funny.

You can not go up.

You can not come down.

And you can not come in.

Modern Curriculum Press Beginning-To-Read Books

Margaret Hillert, author of several books in the MCP Beginning-To-Read Series, is a writer, poet, and teacher.

The Three Little Pigs

The classic nursery story told in just 34 preprimer words with charming illustrations that carry the action of the story.

Word List

7 here
is
a
pig

9 and

10 one
two
three
little
funny

12 see
my
house
it
yellow

13 I
want
to
come
in

14 you
can
not

15 puff
the
down

19 me

20 look
big
red

22 go
away

25 up

26 oh